What-a-Mess

Frank Muir

WHAT-A-MESS
A PICTURE CORGI 0 552 52105 1

PRINTING HISTORY

First published 1977 by Ernest Benn Limited
Picture Corgi edition published 1979
Reprinted 1986

Picture Corgi are published by
Transworld Publishers Ltd.,
61-63 Uxbridge Road,
Ealing, London W5.

Printed in Portugal by Printer Portuguesa

WHAT-A-MESS

Illustrated by Joseph Wright

The puppy's real name was Prince Amir of Kinjan. But he had never heard anybody call him that. Face to face with him for the first time—in fact, *every* time they came face to face with him—people always said, 'Good grief! What a mess!'

His mother was beautiful, tall and sleek, with a silky golden coat. People would lean over the gate and say to each other, 'What a beautiful Afghan hound!' Then they would notice a shapeless bundle of muddy fur doing something peculiar, like eating a tree or trying to dig a hole in a puddle. 'What's *that*?' they would say. 'WHAT A MESS!'

It is not surprising, then, that the puppy grew up believing
that his name *was* What-a-mess.

His mother was kind as well as beautiful. She told him all sorts of things which a growing puppy should know. To walk forwards rather than backwards. Not to sit down in his drinking-water bowl. To lie down before going to sleep so that he wouldn't topple over and hurt himself.

Best of all, to keep very still when the doorbell rang during dinner because the people in the house often left the table unguarded. Then an alert puppy could quickly snatch a bread roll, or a haddock, or — at the very least — the string round the Sunday roast beef.

But his mother did not tell him quite everything. She forgot to tell him that he was a puppy.

'Listen,' he would sometimes say, one foot in his food, as he watched his elegant mother neatly crunching her biscuits, 'what *am* I?' The beautiful Afghan would look in despair at his tangled coat — a mess of rose-bush clippings, jam, burrs, sticky buds and assorted twigs — and sigh, 'You're no puppy of mine, looking like that. What a mess!'

One Monday morning, What-a-mess decided that the time had come to find out what he really was. He had finished his work early — he had barked at the milkman, eaten part of the morning papers, chased the cat, dug a hole in the lawn, patrolled the back hedge and frightened an elderly lady, and gone to sleep twice.

He had quite a long time to spare before his next duty, leaping up and pulling the washing down from the clothes line, so he decided to do a bit of thinking in his Thinking Place, on top of the high hedge at the back of the house. He took a light snack with him, four daffodils and a cardboard box.

'What ever I am,' he wondered, 'I can't be the same sort of thing as my mother. She is tall and slim. I am short and fat. Very short, really, and extremely fat. Now, I shall look around the world carefully. When I find something as short and fat as I am — that will be what I am!'

This brilliant piece of thinking was pleasing, but also tiring, so he closed his eyes and had another snooze.

A bee woke him up. A plump, busy bee which buzzed round his ear before buzzing away and hovering over a marigold. What-a-mess watched the bee vaguely for a while. Then inspiration struck. 'Very short . . . extremely fat . . . I'M A BEE! That's what I am! A big, huge, gigantic BEE!'

He was so excited at his great discovery that he could not wait to begin his new, true life being a bee. It was not easy scrambling to his feet on top of the hedge but he finally managed it.

With a bee-like bark, he launched himself into space towards a distant clump of clover, beating his legs up and down in the air as the bee beat his wings . . .

Five feet is a long way for a fat puppy to drop. His tummy seemed to rise to the back of his mouth. His whole life flashed before him. This did not take long because he was too young for much to have happened in his life, but it was a very nasty feeling. Just when he felt that he had been falling for ever, 'Squodge!' He found himself in the compost heap.

'Well,' he thought to himself an hour later, still trying to get the stickier bits of eggshells, cold porridge and failed meringue out of his coat, 'at least I know I'm not a bee! Thank goodness. I *hate* flying!'

That afternoon, a very large lady came to call about the village rummage sale. What-a-mess hid underneath the sofa because he knew that when ladies came to call in the afternoon, they were usually given a slice of cake. They often put the plate on the floor near the sofa.

He waited for quite a long time, not making a sound. But the
lady did not put her plate of cake down. Instead she took off
her hat and put it on the floor next to where What-a-mess was
hiding. It was a large, wide hat with fur wrapped round the
top. Golden fur, short and fat.

'I'm a hat!' whispered What-a-mess to himself (silently of course). 'I will spend the rest of my life being taken to exciting places on a lady's head! I'm a huge, beautiful HAT!'

Very carefully, so that nobody would notice, he nibbled and nudged the fur away from the hat and took its place, wrapping himself snugly round the brim and curling up tight. Even when a plate of cake *was* suddenly put on the floor an inch away from his nose he didn't move. 'Hats,' he said to himself, 'don't eat cake.'

He did not have long to wait.

'Good-bye!' boomed the large lady in her loud voice. She bent down and swept the hat off the floor and onto her head. The puppy clung tight. Then the lady drew a huge hatpin out of her lapel. She jabbed it into the hat . . .

'YEEEEEEEOOOOOOOAAAAAAAAAOOOWWWKKKK!'
yelped the puppy, rising as if by magic two feet in the air and
crashing down into the tea-things.

During the uproar which followed, the puppy leaped through
legs and made his escape.

He went to the pool under the trees at the end of the garden where he always went when he had done something awful. Sometimes he went there fifteen times a day.

As he lay there, trying to lick his wound through his matted coat, he said to himself, 'Well, I'm not a hat. That's *something* to be glad about — I rather like eating cake. But if I am not a bee, and I'm not a hat — what is there left in the world that I might be?'

He began to feel quite sorry for himself. He even tried a whimper or two to see whether that would cheer him up. It didn't. So he sank his chin on the edge of the pool and gazed into its dark and somewhat smelly depths. There, deep down, he suddenly saw a fish swimming slowly among the weeds. It was a brownish sort of fish, short and fat.

'I'm a FISH!' he yelped in excitement. 'Of course — why didn't I think of that before? I'll spend my time moving lazily along in the cool depths — hey, friend, wait for me!' And folding his front legs back against his body like fishes' fins, he plunged in head-first . . .

It was a nasty shock. Even nastier than dropping into the compost or being speared by the hatpin. The water closed over his head. He couldn't see. He tried to open his eyes but the water hurt. Everything was blurred and cold. He tried to breathe but he only swallowed water which made him choke. As he struggled his feet became tangled in weeds.

He might have been stuck there for ever. But two ducks swam along. Thinking that the puppy was some unknown pond-monster come to frighten their ducklings they pecked him hard, tweaking tufts of fur out of his coat. This pushed him free of the weeds, allowing him to drag himself to safety on the bank.

It was a very messy puppy indeed who curled up in his basket that evening. A puppy with a sore hatpin wound, with bald patches, the beginnings of a cold from his soaking in the pond and a bedraggled coat full of compost, cake-crumbs and pond-weed. For once his beautiful Afghan mother did not sigh and say, 'What-a-mess!' Instead, thinking that he was asleep, she began gently picking bits off him.

'You're a villain,' she whispered as she worked away, 'and an eye-sore, and a one-puppy disaster wherever you go.' She nuzzled him. 'But really, deep down, you're a dear!'

'At last!' What-a-mess said to himself gleefully — he had only been pretending sleep so that his mother would not be cross — 'the real truth about what I am! My mother should know! I'm a deer!'

And so as the various members of the household closed their eyes and drifted off into their dreams, the puppy lay wide awake, his brain racing.

'What sort of deer? I must find out tomorrow.' The only deer he had seen were small and brown so it *was* true. Perhaps the horns would grow later. Big ones to help dig up rose bushes, open tins of food and frighten the cat . . .

It had been a good day to look back on. There was an even better day to look forward to.